小河狸
與
回聲

埃米・麥克唐納 文
薩拉・福克斯戴維斯 圖

This edition published in 1996 by
Magi Publications
22 Manchester Street, London W1M 5PG

First published in Great Britain in 1990 by
Walker Books Ltd, London

Printed and bound in Italy

ISBN 1 85430 507 7

Little Beaver and The Echo

Written by Amy MacDonald
Illustrated by Sarah Fox-Davies

Translated by East Word

小河狸獨自一人住在一池塘邊上。
他沒有兄弟姐妹，更糟的是：他連一個朋友也沒有。
一天，他坐在池塘邊哭起來，而且越哭音聲越大。

Little Beaver lived all alone by the edge of a big pond.
He didn't have any brothers. He didn't have any sisters.
Worst of all, he didn't have any friends.
One day, sitting by the side of the pond, he began to cry.
He cried out loud. Then he cried out louder.

突然，他聽到一種很怪的聲音。在池塘的對面，
也有哭泣之聲。小河狸不哭了，靜下來聽著……
對面的哭聲也停止了。
小河狸又孤單了。
“嗚!”他喊道。
池塘對面傳來“嗚!”的喊聲。
“哇!”小河狸又喊。
池塘對面傳來“哇!”的喊聲。

Suddenly he heard something very strange. On the
other side of the pond, someone else was crying too.
Little Beaver stopped crying and listened.
The other crying stopped.
Little Beaver was alone again.
“Booo hooo,” he said.
“Booo hooo,” said the voice from across the pond.
“Huh-huh-waaah!” said Little Beaver.
“Huh-huh-waaah!” said the voice from across the pond.

小河狸停止了哭泣，“喂!”他喊道。
池塘對面傳來“喂!”的聲音。
“你因爲甚麼事哭呀？”小河狸問。
池塘對面的聲音問: “你因爲甚麼事哭呀？”
小河狸想了想，說: “我很孤獨，我想找個朋友。”
池塘對面回答: “我很孤獨，我想找個朋友。”

Little Beaver stopped crying. “Hello!” he called.
“Hello!” said the voice from across the pond.
“Why are you crying?” asked Little Beaver.
“Why are you crying?” asked the voice from across the pond.
Little Beaver thought for a moment. “I’m lonely,” he said. “I need a friend.”
“I’m lonely,” said the voice from across the pond.
“I need a friend.”

小河狸不相信池塘對岸住著和他一樣孤獨，
也需要找朋友的人。
他馬上乘上小船，出發尋找。

Little Beaver couldn't believe it. On the other side of the pond lived somebody else who was sad and needed a friend.
He got right into his boat and set off to find him.

這是個很大的池塘。小河狸划著划著……
突然發現一隻小鴨子獨自在水裡打轉。
小河狸說: “我正在尋找位需要朋友的人，
剛才哭的是你嗎？”
鴨子說: “我的確需要朋友，但剛才不是我在哭。”
小河狸說: “把我當你的朋友，上來吧。”
於是鴨子跳上了小船。

It was a big pond. He paddled and paddled. Then he saw a young duck, swimming in circles all by himself.
“I'm looking for someone who needs a friend,” said Little Beaver. “Was it *you* who was crying?”
“I do need a friend,” said the duck. “But it wasn't me who was crying.”
“I'll be your friend,” said Little Beaver. “Come with me.”
So the duck jumped into the boat.